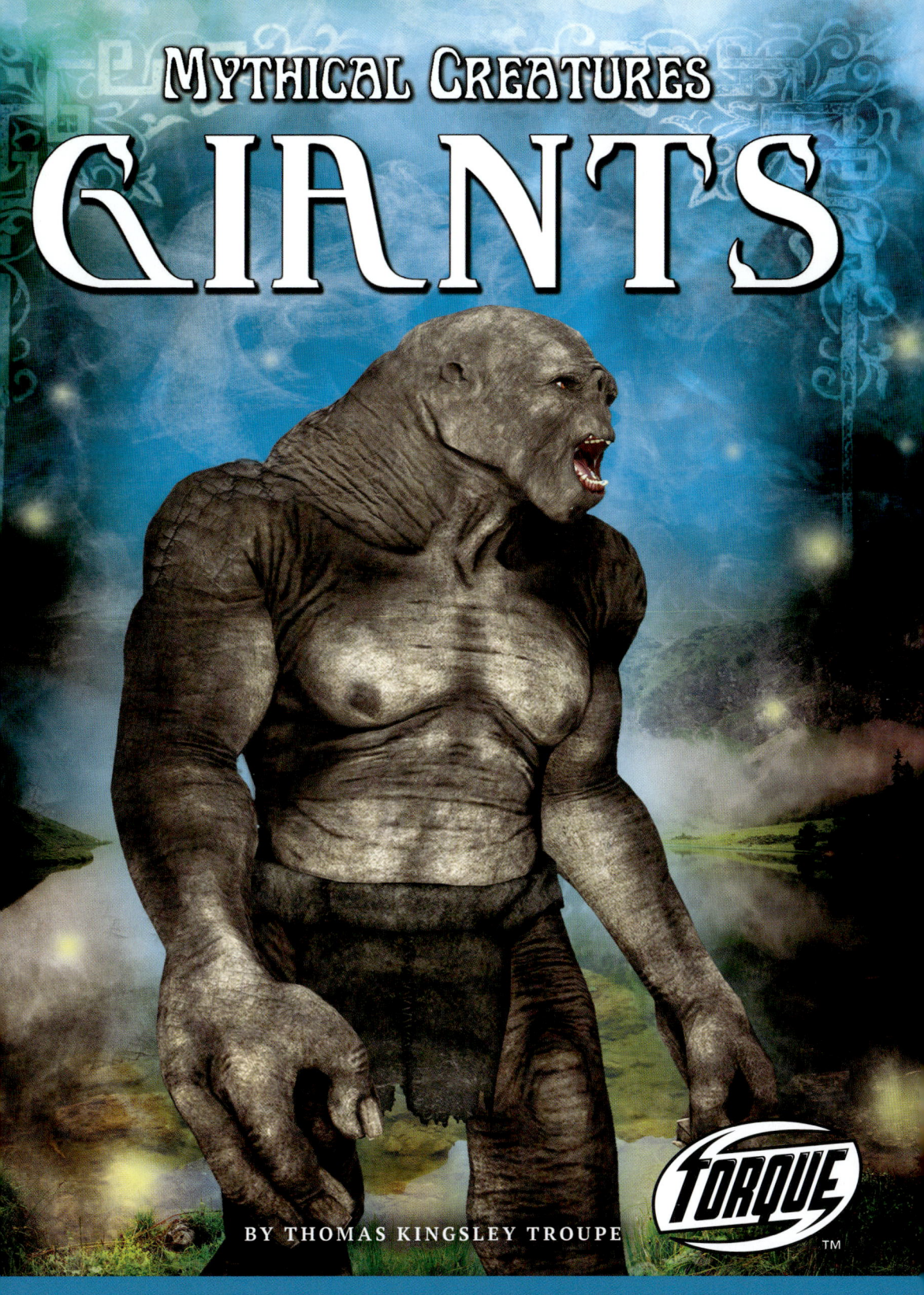

# MYTHICAL CREATURES
# GIANTS

BY THOMAS KINGSLEY TROUPE

BELLWETHER MEDIA • MINNEAPOLIS, MN

**Torque** brims with excitement perfect for thrill-seekers of all kinds. Discover daring survival skills, explore uncharted worlds, and marvel at mighty engines and extreme sports. In *Torque* books, anything can happen. Are you ready?

This edition first published in 2021 by Bellwether Media, Inc.

No part of this publication may be reproduced in whole or in part without written permission of the publisher.
For information regarding permission, write to Bellwether Media, Inc., Attention: Permissions Department,
6012 Blue Circle Drive, Minnetonka, MN 55343.

Library of Congress Cataloging-in-Publication Data

Names: Troupe, Thomas Kingsley, author.
Title: Giants / by Thomas Kingsley Troupe.
Description: Minneapolis, MN : Bellwether Media, 2021. | Series: Torque | Includes bibliographical references and index. | Audience: Ages 7-12 | Audience: Grades 4-6 | Summary: "Engaging images accompany information about giants. The combination of high-interest subject matter and light text is intended for students in grades 3 through 7"-Provided by publisher.
Identifiers: LCCN 2020014900 (print) | LCCN 2020014901 (ebook) | ISBN 9781644872741 | ISBN 9781681037370 (ebook)
Subjects: LCSH: Giants–Juvenile literature.
Classification: LCC GR560 .K56 2021 (print) | LCC GR560 (ebook) | DDC 398/.45–dc23
LC record available at https://lccn.loc.gov/2020014900
LC ebook record available at https://lccn.loc.gov/2020014901

Text copyright © 2021 by Bellwether Media, Inc. TORQUE and associated logos are trademarks and/or registered trademarks of Bellwether Media, Inc.

Editor: Rebecca Sabelko    Designer: Josh Brink

Printed in the United States of America, North Mankato, MN.

# TABLE OF CONTENTS

| | |
|---|---|
| THE LEGENDS OF GIANTS | 4 |
| GIANT LORE | 10 |
| TODAY'S GIANTS | 18 |
| GLOSSARY | 22 |
| TO LEARN MORE | 23 |
| INDEX | 24 |

# THE LEGENDS OF GIANTS

A bus-sized foot stomps down. The ground shakes. The giant just misses you. You hide behind a tree. The giant begins to pull trees from the ground. Dirt rains down from the roots. You run away, but the giant follows you. Its booming footsteps shake the forest floor. Will the giant catch you?

### REAL-LIFE GIANT
Today's definition of a giant is a person who is over 7 feet (2 meters) tall.

Giants have appeared in **myths**, art, and **legends** since ancient times. Their stories are found in **cultures** around the world.

Some stories tell of giants who roamed the earth long before humans came along. They were creatures born from the gods. The giants lived in the mountains and ate raw meat. Their battles with the gods shaped the landscape into mountains and seas.

In stories, many giants look like humans with huge bodies. Some giants are a few feet taller than people. Others are as tall as buildings. They have snakes for legs in Greek myths.

Some giants are friendly. But many are mean and scary monsters. They are easy to outwit. Heroes rarely need to use their strength to defeat them.

Greek giant

# GIANT LORE

Kumbhakarna

Tales about giants have been told for thousands of years. They appear in many religions. Giants in the Jewish and Christian Bibles were often greedy and dangerous.

The Hindu giant Kumbhakarna was loyal. But he could not control his appetite. He ate everything in sight, even humans!

## Giant Origin

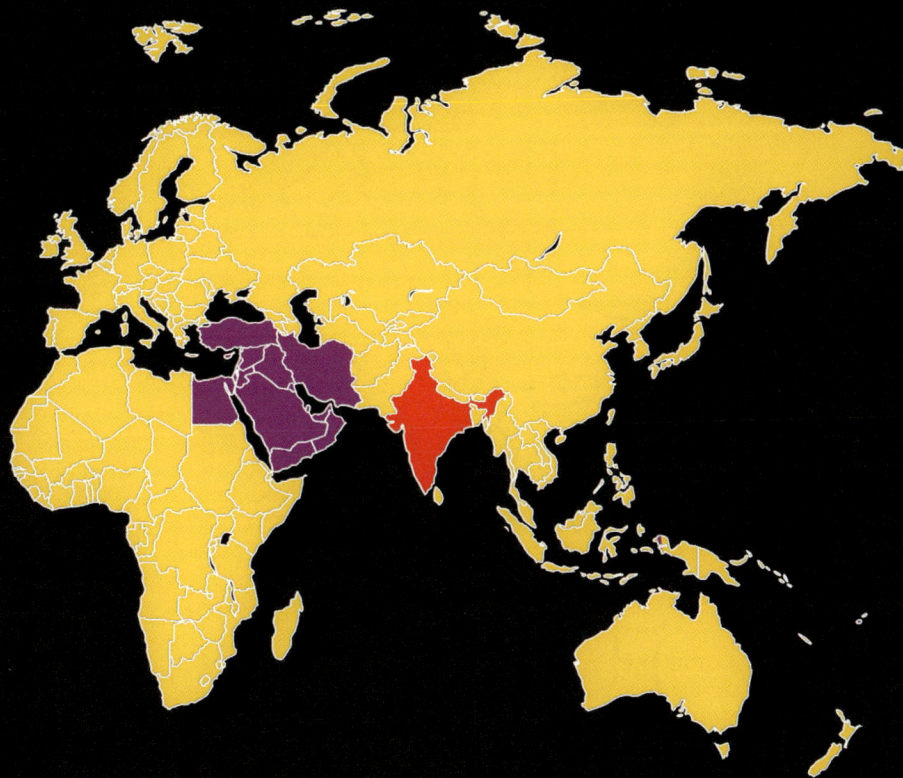

**Middle East (Judaism and Christianity)** =
**India (Hinduism)** =

During the 1900s, giants became helpful heroes in American **folklore**. Paul Bunyan was a friendly **lumberjack** who ate huge pancakes. He cleared forests with one swing of his axe.

The story of John Henry was based on a real person. He was a huge man who smashed more rock than a machine. He became a hero for American workers.

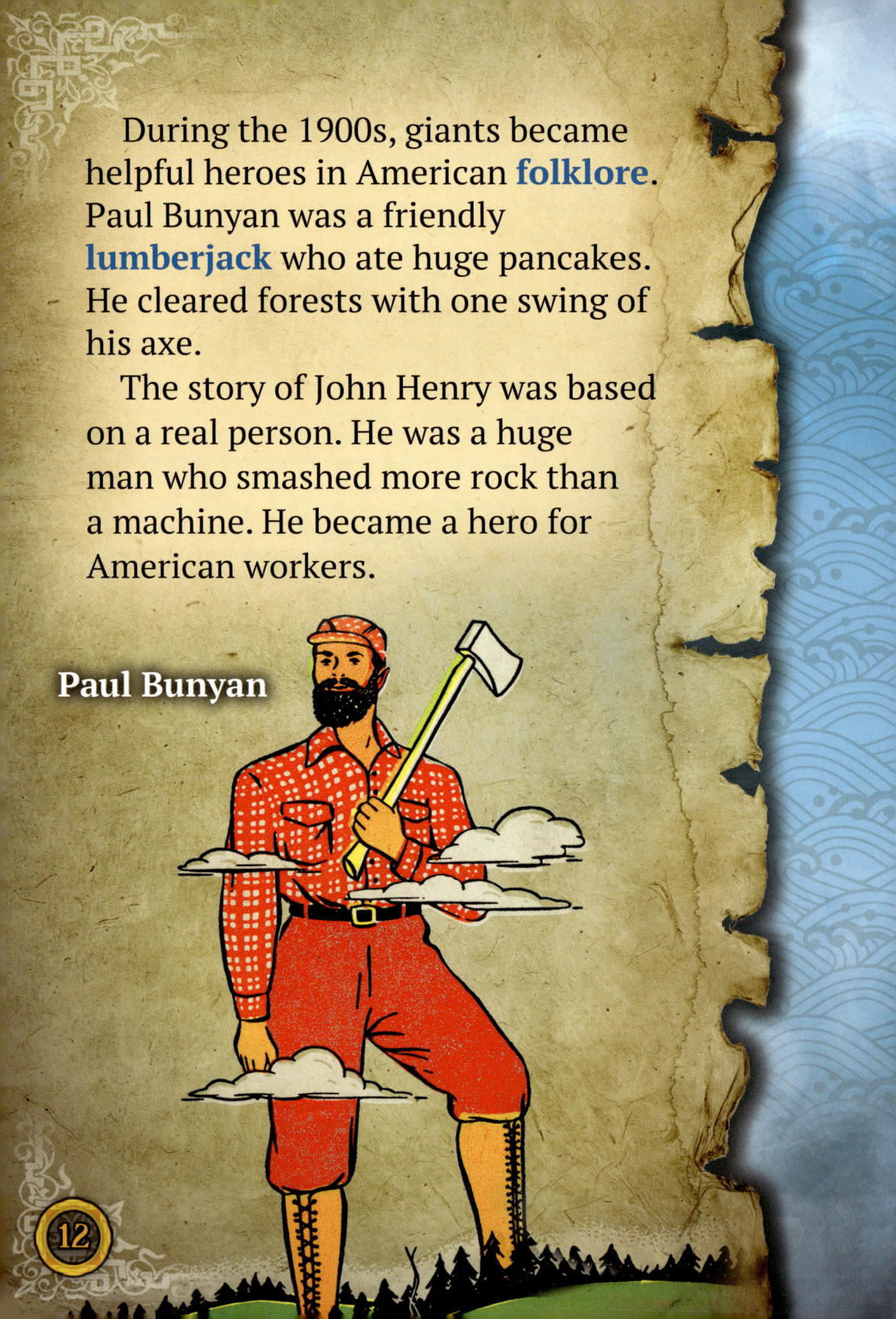

Paul Bunyan

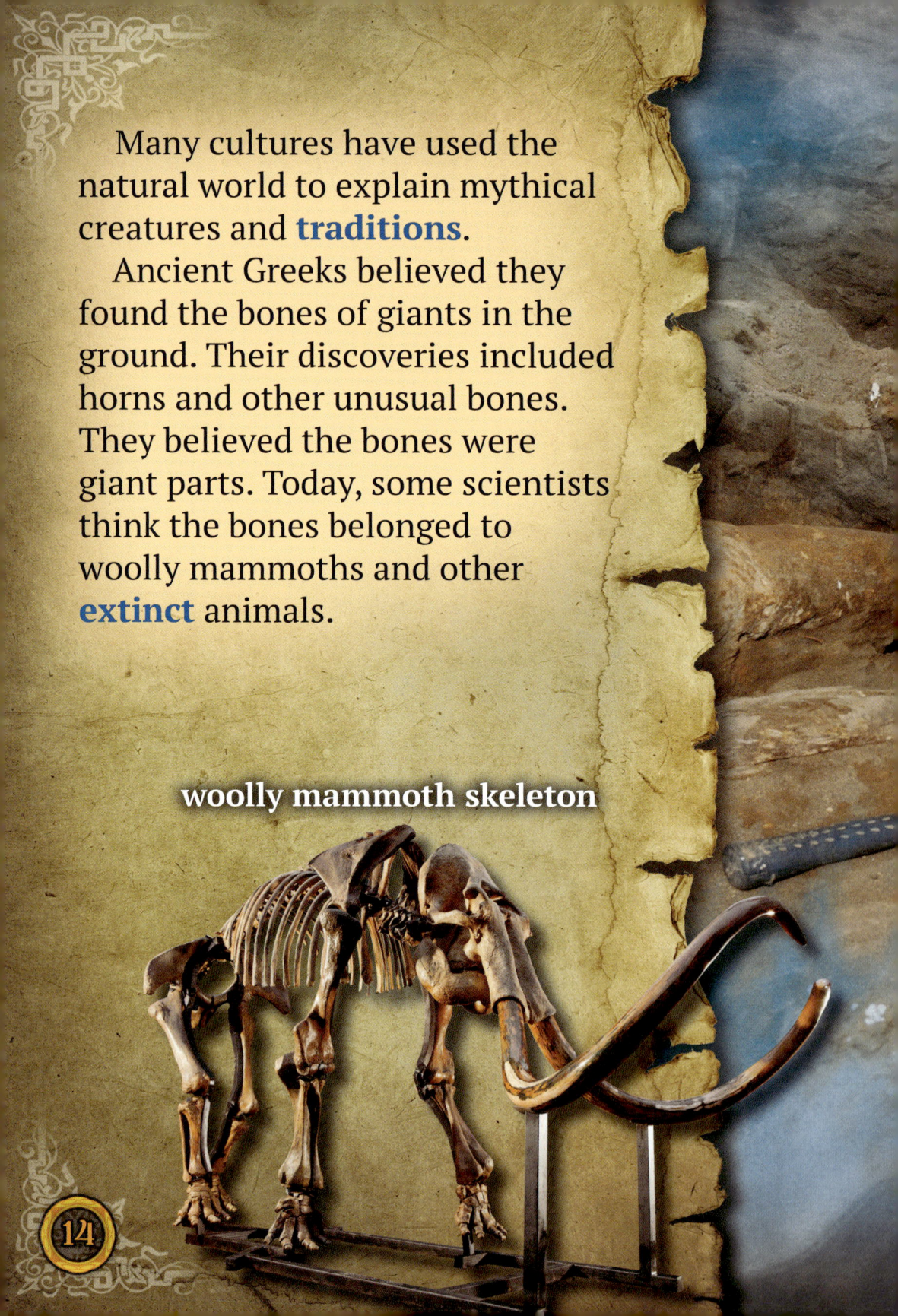

Many cultures have used the natural world to explain mythical creatures and **traditions**.

Ancient Greeks believed they found the bones of giants in the ground. Their discoveries included horns and other unusual bones. They believed the bones were giant parts. Today, some scientists think the bones belonged to woolly mammoths and other **extinct** animals.

**woolly mammoth skeleton**

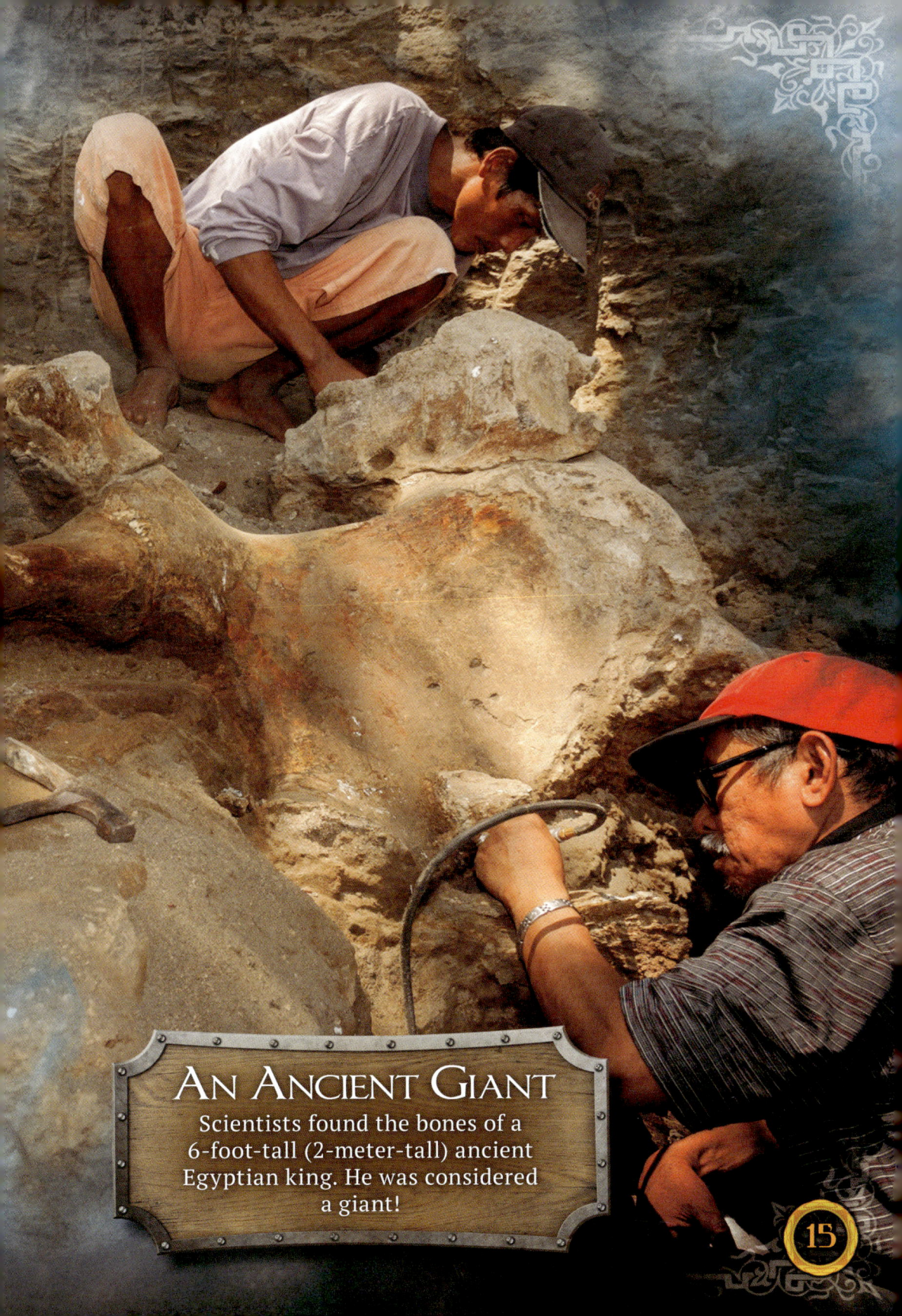

## An Ancient Giant

Scientists found the bones of a 6-foot-tall (2-meter-tall) ancient Egyptian king. He was considered a giant!

Not all giants are from tall tales. Robert Wadlow was the tallest man in the world. He was almost 9 feet (3 meters) tall! His height was due to high levels of the human growth **hormone**.

Robert had a hard life. People stared at him because of his size. But people from his hometown loved him. He was often called "the gentle giant."

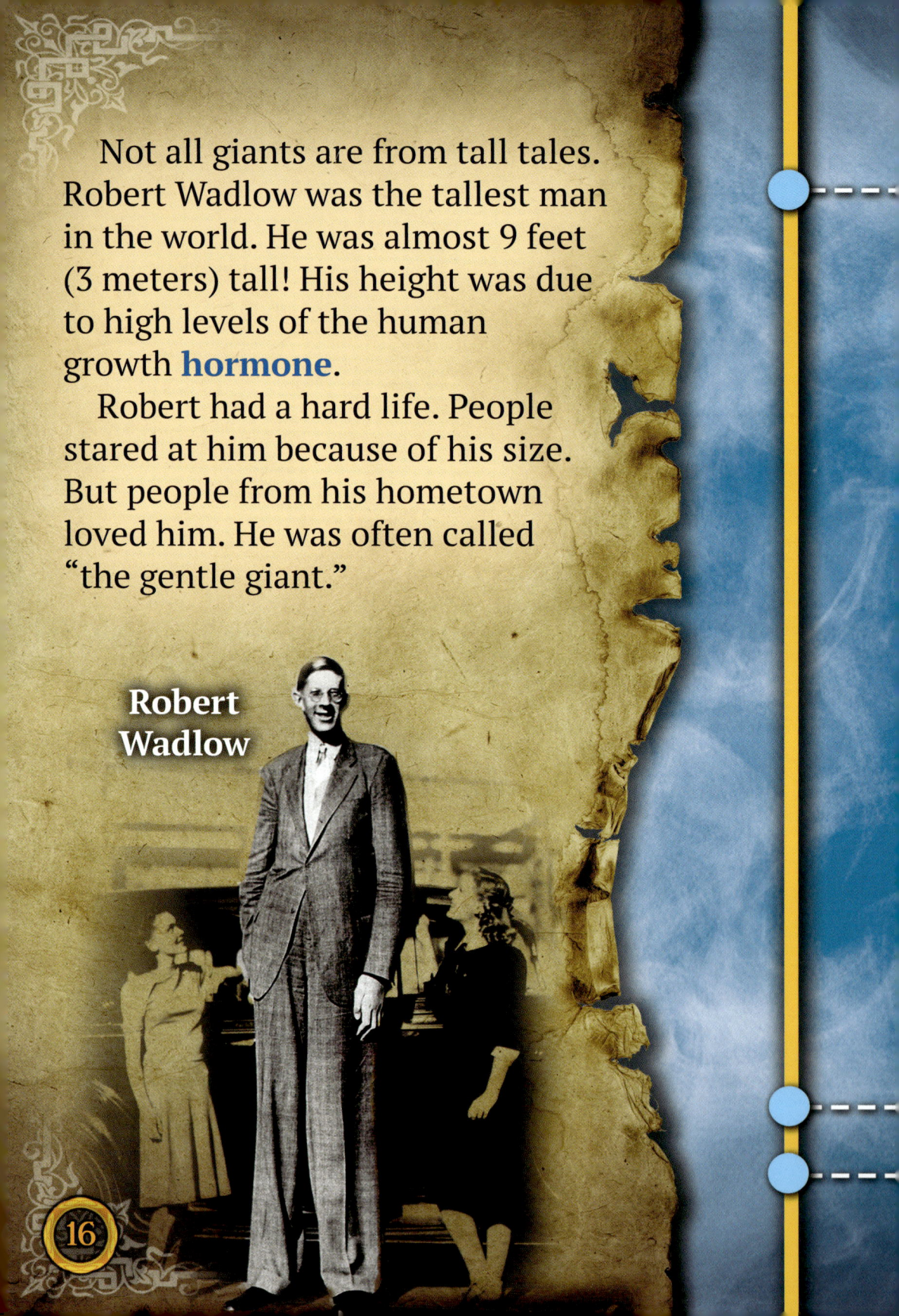

Robert Wadlow

# Giant Timeline

**1200 to 165 BCE:** Stories about giants are written in the Jewish and Christian Bibles

**1906:** First Paul Bunyan story is printed

**1918:** Robert Wadlow is born and later becomes the tallest man in the world

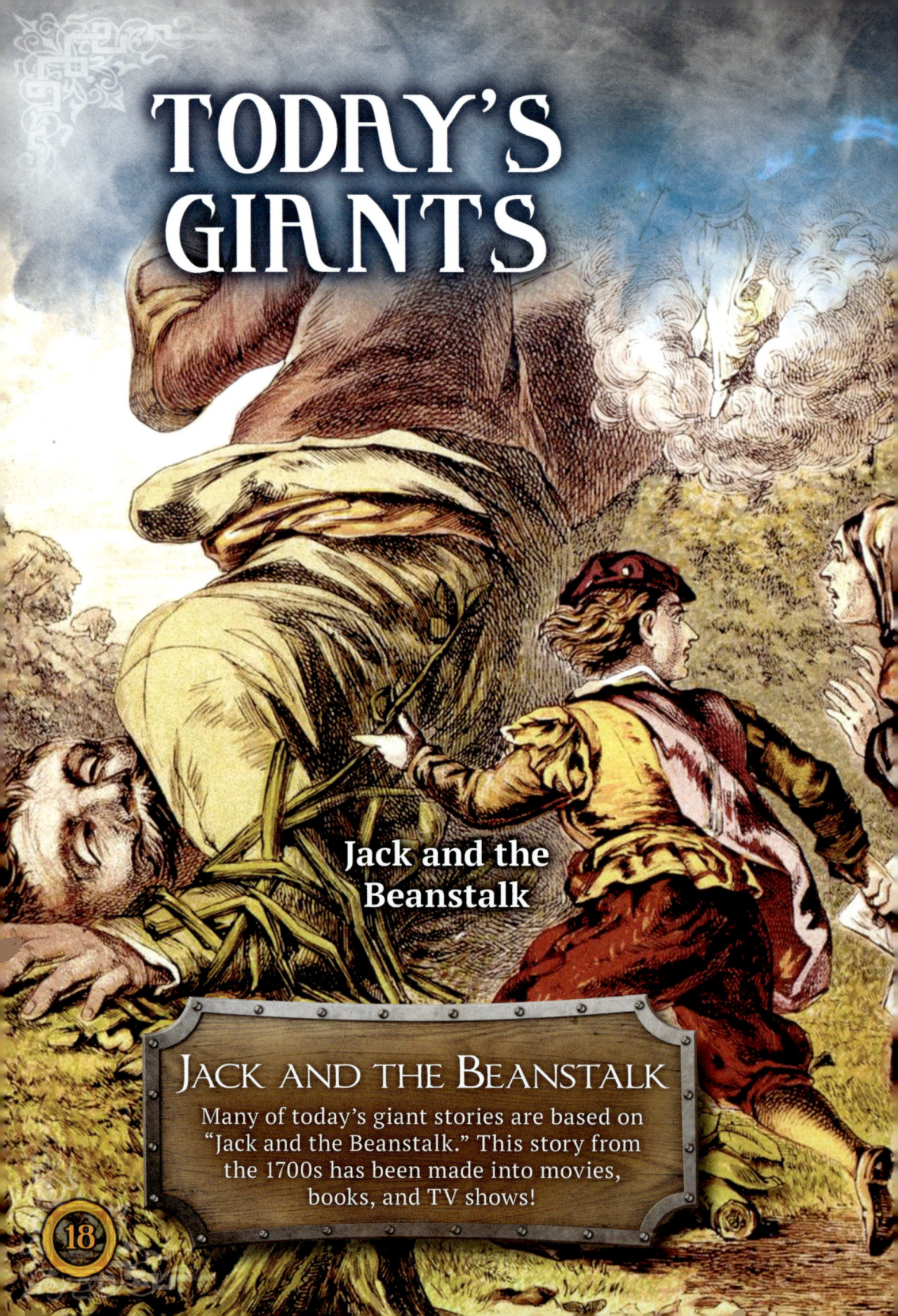

# Today's Giants

## Jack and the Beanstalk

### Jack and the Beanstalk

Many of today's giant stories are based on "Jack and the Beanstalk." This story from the 1700s has been made into movies, books, and TV shows!

Giants continue to stomp their way into today's world. Companies like Green Giant use the creature in a positive way to sell products. The Jolly Green Giant makes vegetables seem fun and magical.

But giants also appear as large and mean. Both the National Football League and Major League Baseball include teams named after the feared monsters.

**Jolly Green Giant**

Video games, books, and movies feature giants, too! The book and film *The BFG* are about a friendly giant. The story teaches people not to judge others based on how they look. The video game *Shadow of the Colossus* has 16 stone giants that must be defeated.

Whether **depicted** as gentle or frightening, giants still play a big part in our world!

Shadow of the Colossus

# Media Mention

**Movie:** *The Iron Giant*

**Year Released:** 1999

**Summary:** A young boy becomes friends with a giant space robot. They work together to keep the government from destroying the Iron Giant.

## The BFG

# GLOSSARY

**cultures**—the beliefs, values, and ways of life of groups of people

**depicted**—described using words or shown in a picture

**extinct**—no longer living

**folklore**—the customs, beliefs, stories, and sayings of a group of people

**hormone**—a substance that is made in the body that affects the way the body grows

**legends**—stories from the past that are believed by many people but cannot be proved to be true

**lumberjack**—someone who cuts down trees for a living

**myths**—ancient stories about the beliefs or history of a group of people; myths also try to explain events.

**traditions**—customs, ideas, or beliefs handed down from one generation to the next

# TO LEARN MORE

## AT THE LIBRARY

Lawrence, Sandra, and Stuart Hill. *The Atlas of Monsters: Mythical Creatures from Around the World*. Philadelphia, Pa.: Running Press Kids, 2019.

London, Martha. *Giants*. Minneapolis, Minn.: Pop!, 2020.

Peebles, Alice. *Giants and Trolls*. Minneapolis, Minn.: Hungry Tomato, 2016.

## ON THE WEB

Factsurfer.com gives you a safe, fun way to find more information.

1. Go to www.factsurfer.com

2. Enter "giants" into the search box and click 🔍.

3. Select your book cover to see a list of related content.

# INDEX

appearance, 8
around the world, 13
art, 7
*BFG, The*, 20, 21
Bibles, 10
bones, 14, 15
Bunyan, Paul, 12
cultures, 7, 14
explanations, 14
folklore, 12
gods, 7
Greek, 8, 14
Green Giant, 18
Henry, John, 12
history, 10, 11, 12
humans, 7, 8, 11, 16
*Iron Giant, The*, 21
Jack and the Beanstalk, 18
*Jotuns*, 9
Kumbhakarna, 10, 11
legends, 7
Major League Baseball, 18
mountains, 7
myths, 7, 8, 9, 13
National Football League, 18
origin, 11
religions, 10, 11
*Shadow of the Colossus*, 20
size, 4, 8, 15, 16
timeline, 16-17
traditions, 14
Wadlow, Robert, 16

The images in this book are reproduced through the courtesy of: tsuneomp, front cover (hero); Smileus, front cover (background); Vuk Kostic, p. 3; Miki Pavlovikj, pp. 4-5; Hilary Morgan/ Alamy, pp. 6-7; Chronicle/ Alamy, p. 7; Olaf Krüger/ Alamy, p. 8; British Library/ Alamy, pp. 9, 10; CSA-Printstock, pp. 12, 17 (bottom); Isabel Poulin, p. 13 (bottom left); The History Collection/ Alamy, p. 13 (bottom right)(top left); Artokoloro/ Alamy, p. 13 (top right); Beatrissa, p. 14; Reynold Sumayku/ Alamy, pp. 14-15; Science History Images/ Alamy, p. 16; GL Archive/ Alamy, p. 17 (top); Smith Archive/ Alamy, pp. 18-19; Jacob Sabelko, p. 20; TCD/Prod. DB/ Alamy, pp. 20-21; Raggedstone, p. 22; Daniel Eskridge, p. 22 (giant).